CW00863460

Muscles and Brains

Two Mice From Staines

Muscles and Brains © Copyright 2004 by Norman Bailey

Illustrations © Kevin Bolton

All rights reserved. No part of this work may be reproduced or stored in an information retrieval system (other than for purposes of review) without prior written permission by the copyright holder.

A catalogue record of this book is available from the British Library

First Edition: December 2004

ISBN: 1-84375-123-2

This is a work of fiction. Names, characters, places and incidents are the product of the author's imagination or are used fictitiously, and any resemblance to any actual persons, living or dead, events, or locales is entirely coincidental.

To order additional copies of this book please visit:
http://www.upso.co.uk/normanbailey

Published by: UPSO Ltd
5 Stirling Road, Castleham Business Park,
St Leonards-on-Sea, East Sussex TN38 9NW United Kingdom
Tel: 01424 853349 Fax: 0870 191 3991
Email: info@upso.co.uk   Web: http://www.upso.co.uk

Muscles and Brains
Two Mice From Staines

by

Norman Bailey

Illustrated by
Kevin Bolton

UPSO

I would like to dedicate this book to my Grandfather, Edward (Ted) Penman. He was the kindest, most wonderful man that I have ever known. He worked in Staines Linoleum for 45 years. On weekends he often took me down to the Thames to fee the swans and ducks near Staines Bridge. They were such wonderful days. It has changed very little in the past 50 years.

Also many thanks to Sharon for all her hard work and Kevin for producing the illustrations in such short time.

Introduction

Having been abruptly moved from the warm, safe home they shared with their parents and siblings in a garden shed in Staines, Muscles and Brains found themselves in a strange, frightening place far out in the country with no one to look after them.

On their own, neither could meet the challenges of finding his way home, but together after an accidental surge of electricity, they became a pair of super mice. Muscles having the strength to overcome physical obstacles and Brains the intelligence to come up with solutions to any problem they encountered.

Their journey to reunite with their family in Staines takes them on adventures they had never imagined. From escaping huge and obviously hungry creatures, humans who didn't want them around and to using their new found powers to help others, Muscles and Brains make their way with imagination and ingenuity. Muscles and Brains - Two Mice From Staines is packed full of excitement, humour and flights of fancy from cover to cover.

Chapter One

In The Beginning

At the bottom of a garden somewhere in Staines stood a garden shed. In this shed was a tea chest full of all sorts of household stuff. It had stood in the corner untouched for years. In the bottom amongst cups, saucers, etc., and some ripped up paper there was a bundle of young bodies. Their eyes were just open, they all had some fur. They were the offspring of Mr. and Mrs. Penmouse. They had used this same shed for several years now and quite a few baby mice had started their lives here.

Mr. and Mrs. Penmouse are just ordinary mice and want no more out of life than any other creatures. Just enough food to eat, enough water to drink and somewhere warm and safe to bring up their babies. This had been the way of things for a long time now. But all that was about to change. The people who lived in the house nearby and owned the land around the shed had decided to move away. Now they were clearing their belongings and putting them on a big lorry. The tea chest was the last thing to be taken. Thank goodness Peter and Penny Penmouse had seen what was happening. They started to get their babies out of the tea chest and into a safer place underneath the shed. But before they could get the last two out, the chest was lifted into the air and taken away. The man put it on to the back of the lorry, shut the doors and drove off. Peter and Penny were crying at the loss of their two babies but knew that they had got the strongest babies to safety. They were not sure that the two left behind would survive very long even before this tragedy happened, but now without any chance to look after them, to feed them, they were sure that within a few hours they would be dead.

The lorry arrived at a house deep in the country in a small village. Soon the lorry was being emptied and all the furniture and boxes of human belongings were being put inside a very, very old house.

The tea chest was thrown into a cupboard

under the stairs. It landed next to a box hanging on the wall with lots of old electric wires attached to it. The tea chest had knocked one of these wires out and the end landed inside the box next to the two baby mice. Of course, they didn't know anything about wires and electric or they would have been very worried indeed.

This house was very, very old and the wiring had been here for many years. Also, the house had been left empty for years with no heating on. Some pipes in the loft had burst and water had poured down the walls. If the humans flicked the switch to put the electric on, they would be in serious trouble. Of course, the mice would be as well.

When the lorry had been emptied and was driven away, the new owners of this old house decided to try and get some of the furniture in the correct rooms. But first they had to clean up. There was mess everywhere.

Several hours and a lot of sweeping, dusting and cleaning later, the two humans needed a rest and, of course, a nice cup of tea. When they tried to boil the kettle they realized that the electricity was switched off. Oh dear! One of them went to the cupboard under the stairs and opened the electricity box to check the fuses. He noticed that the ON/OFF lever was pointing towards OFF. So he grabbed hold of it and pulled it up into the ON position. There was one very loud BANG and the human was thrown backwards out of the cupboard. He had been shocked but was fortunate because the electricity threw him away from the wires.

The two baby mice in the tea chest were both given a massive jolt of electricity. It went from the tips of their tails to the tips of their noses. Now normally this amount of electricity would have killed most creatures. Even humans have been killed by such a massive blast through their bodies. But somehow this time, for whatever reason, they didn't die. Instead of killing them, the shock had a strange but marvelous effect on them both. You must remember that these are two weak baby mice that were not expected to live very long. But all of a sudden immediately after the shock, the pair of them seemed to have a new and wonderful lease of life. Both of them seemed so much stronger. Their fur had grown suddenly thicker and they both seemed much stronger.

One of them shouted to the other, "We must get out of here. Follow me." He started to climb over the cups and other things that were all around the nest. The other one followed without question. Somehow he knew not to query his brother's orders. When they looked up, they realized that the top of the chest was just out of their reach. The sides were too slippery to climb. What could they do? How were they going to get out?

Just then one of them said, "What we need to do is for one of us to stand on the other one's shoulders so we can reach the top. If you get up there, do you think you can pull me up? I don't think I'm strong enough to pull you up."

"Sure I can. Let me get on your shoulders so we can get out of here."

In no time at all he was on top of the tea chest and was reaching down for his brother. Soon both of them were balancing on top and were looking for a way down to the floor.

"It's a long way down, too far for us to jump."

"Don't worry," said his brother. "I can jump down, but how am I going to get you down as well?"

Just then, one brother said, "Look, over there. Can you see that box full of wool? If you can bring some a bit nearer I can jump down on to it. The wool will help break my fall. I'll chance it if you get it near enough."

So down his brother went. He landed on the floor and rolled over, landing on his feet, safe and sound. Instead of getting into the shoe box full of wool and taking some for his brother to jump on to, he just pushed the whole box.

"It's not heavy," he shouted. "There we are. Now, jump on to that and let's get out of here." His brother was soon on his way to a soft wooly landing.

"How could you push that heavy box?" he asked. "It would be too heavy for me to shift." His brother just smiled and said, "You seem to come up with the good ideas and I seem to be able to do the heavy work. I don't know how we do it, but we can and do. We need names so how about from now on we call each other Muscles and Brains?

They were soon running out of the house and down the garden path, hopefully to a safer place. Oh how they wished it was a safer place. But to mice, there is no such thing as a safe place for very long.

Chapter Two

The Cat

They came across a familiar sight. It was a shed. Somehow they associated the shed with home and safety. Soon they were standing by what seemed to them to be a huge door. Well, you must remember that they are only little mice.

"How are we going to get in there?" asked Muscles. "Let's have a look all around in case there is a hole that we can squeeze through," said Brains.

After a good look all around they saw that there were no holes and no windows to climb through.

Just then the shed door opened and out stepped a man with a spade in his hand. He didn't seem to see them as they ran between his feet and into the shed. They saw the door close behind them and were pleased that the man was now outside. They decided to explore all around the shed for food and shelter, but also to see if there was any danger about such as a cat or a mouse trap. Brains told Muscles what to look out for as they searched high and low until they had looked around the whole shed.

"All clear!" said Brains out loud. "Yes! I think so," squeaked Muscles. "Good. Let's go back to that bag of grain I found and have some supper, then we'll build a bed in that box of old rags that you found." "OK, good idea. I'm so hungry I could eat a cat," laughed Muscles. So they ate and fell asleep in the box of old rags.

They were woken up a few hours later by the man as he came back with the spade. They stayed still and quiet where they lay in case they were seen. Humans don't like mice around and would soon chase them away, or worse still, they might kill them.

Some seeds had fallen on to the floor through the hole that Muscles had chewed in the side of the bag. The man spotted the hole and the seeds and was furious. The two mice heard him shouting angrily. He was determined to catch the culprits and kill them. He stomped out of the shed and slammed the door.

They knew that they had no way of getting

out of the shed at the moment and were worried just what the man was going to do. A few minutes later he came back and started putting strange contraptions on the floor near the grain. He put down four of them and then went out the door, locking it behind him.

"Don't go near those," shouted Brains. "They're dangerous and can kill you if you step on them."

"But they have my favourite food on them," complained Muscles. He was so upset because there were peanuts on the traps and he just loved peanuts.

Before Brains could stop him, he had picked up one of the traps and had thrown it against the shed wall. "Snap" went the trap. Fortunately, neither of them were anywhere near it.

"Right!" said Muscles. "Now we can have the peanuts, then I'll do the same with the other three. We'll eat well tonight."

That night they slept soundly but the next morning was not going to be a good one at all.

Just after daybreak they heard the man coming down the path towards the shed. He opened the door and stepped in. They would have run through his legs and got as far away as possible, but just as they were about to do so, Brains spotted something terrible. Something so dangerous that he couldn't move. He was glued to the spot. He noticed that Muscles was just about to make a run for it when he managed somehow to shout to him to stop.

"It's a cat," he squeaked in a fearful voice. "Don't go out there because he'll kill you in seconds."

Muscles quickly turned around and grabbed Brains by the tail, then he pulled him to safety behind some plant pots on the floor. They were very lucky the man was busy examining the mouse traps that he had set. He couldn't understand how the traps had been moved and where all of the peanuts had gone, especially as none of the traps had mice in them. He seemed very disappointed and quite angry because of this. He stormed out of the shed and they heard him call the cat. "Come here Tiddles," he called. "There you are, nice pussy. I have a job for you to do."

"Oh no!" yelled Brains. "He's going to bring the cat in here to catch us. We're doomed for sure. That cat will smell us out and kill us with those huge paws or his sharp teeth. What are we going to do Muscles?"

Muscles didn't say a word. He was already

gathering the traps together. "How can we use these against the cat?" he thought. "What's your plan to beat him?" "I have an idea. Perhaps we can use the mouse traps to stop that cat."

Brains told Muscles to re-set the traps but not to bother putting any bait on them as that would not be necessary. Then he told Muscles to move them behind the flower pots where they had hidden earlier. Brains would have helped but they were too heavy for him.

They heard the shed door open again and saw the cat being put down on the floor and the door was shut. Muscles grabbed Brains and pulled him behind the flower pots, but not before the cat spotted them.

"Meow, meow!" said the cat as he pounced across the shed floor towards them. "Come to me, I'm hungry," he said.

But Muscles and Brains were already trying to get some distance between the cat and themselves. They needed him to follow them so their plan would work.

The cat followed them, not around the pots as they had gone, but sort of over and through them. Not a good move on his part really because as his feet landed, he hit the mouse traps that had been put there by the mice.

Now the cat was jumping all over the place in agony. On each paw he had a mouse trap.

The man heard the commotion and thought the cat had got the mice. He opened the shed door and stepped inside. As soon as the door opened Muscles and Brains were through it and heading up the garden path. Soon they were quite a distance away and felt much safer.

They spotted a garage that happened to have the doors open, so they crept inside for awhile, just in case the man with the cat followed them.

Once inside, they decided to check the place out to look for a safe place to hide and to look for food and water. They stayed in the garage for hours and hours, partly because there was no one else around and, of course, because they found some food and water.

The humans that owned this garage had stored lots of things all around the walls, the shelves and benches. It was full of human stuff. Boxes and boxes of toys were stored here as well as loads of old tools. There were shovels, rakes, pitch forks and other tools hanging on the walls on one side of the garage. Why do humans keep such a load of very old stuff that they hardly ever use?

After exploring for what seemed like

forever they stopped for a meal. They ate sandwiches that had been left on one of the benches and had a drink from a cup full of fizzy pop. They felt very tired, so now seemed like a good time to get some sleep. They had not seen any humans around, or the cat either, so this seemed a very safe place for now. Muscles had uncovered a toy car that was big enough for both of them to sleep in. It was the sort that humans used with remote controls. The seats were very comfortable so they laid across them and went to sleep, Muscles in the back and Brains in the front.

Chapter Three

The Big Escape

Sometime later they were awoken by the sound of humans talking. The voices sounded quite close so they decided to check just how close they were.

The toy car that had been their bed was under a bench. Fortunately, they had pulled a woolen blanket over it so they couldn't be seen from where the humans were standing. They had found the blanket in an old doll house stored nearby.

Unfortunately for them, today was the day when the humans had decided to have a clear out of all their unnecessary rubbish. A lorry turned up outside and left a huge skip by the garage door. Then the two humans started taking some of the boxes of rubbish and throwing it into the skip.

"What a time to have a sort out," moaned Brains. "Couldn't this wait until another day?"

Just as they thought things couldn't get any worse, one of the humans picked up their car(and themselves as they were still laying on the seats). The blanket fell on to the floor and now they were staring at a pair of very scared human eyes. The human lady immediately dropped the car (and them) on to some boxes before it landed with a thump on the garage floor. Fortunately, when the car hit the ground they were thrown out and landed on the soft woolen blanket.

Immediately upon seeing the two mice, the lady screamed at the top of her voice. Why do they always do that? This, of course, attracted the man who was helping her. He ran over to her to see what the problem was.

She pointed to the mice and once more let out an awful scream. The man grabbed a pitch fork that was hanging on the wall and started towards Muscles and Brains.

Brains shouted to Muscles to try and keep the man busy while he tried to hot-wire the car.

"I didn't know you could do that," said Muscles. "Nor did I!" cried Brains excitedly.

"But if we don't get away fast we'll be stuck on that pitch fork."

The human thrust the fork towards Brains but he was already running towards the car. Then the human thrust it at Muscles who just seemed to be waiting to get pierced on one of the prongs. Then, just as it reached him, he stepped to one side and at the same time grabbed the prong nearest to him. The human tried to pull it away but Muscles held on for dear life. The human couldn't believe that there was only a mouse struggling with him. The lady came over to help him and now Muscles was in a spot of bother. He quickly snatched at the pitch fork and he managed to loosen the man's grip on the handle before the lady could help him.

Immediately he spun the pitch fork around so that he was holding the handle the best he could with such small paws, and the prongs faced the two humans. The look on their faces was first one of amazement and then of horror, especially when they saw the pitch fork being held by a tiny mouse coming towards them.

They immediately turned and ran out of the garage as fast as their legs would carry them.

The lady was, of course, screaming at the top of her voice.

Muscles dropped the pitch fork and ran to the toy car to see how Brains was doing. Just as he got there, he heard the car engine roar sweetly. "Got it! I think I've got it!" shouted Brains as his head popped up from beneath the car's bonnet, bumping it with an "Ouch, that hurt."

"Quick Muscles, get in. NO, not that side. You can't drive can you?" Muscles reply was that no he couldn't drive.

"Well, move over and let me then," cut in Brains sharply. "We haven't got much time. Those humans will soon be back and I don't think they'll be very friendly."

Muscles moved to the passenger seat and was amazed that Brains got the car moving within seconds of taking the wheel.

"Just one question," Muscles asked quietly. "Can we go forward please? Going backwards will be more difficult because you won't be able to see where you're going."

Brains just stared at him as he fiddled with the gear levers. Suddenly the car stopped going backwards and shot forwards at quite a fast speed. Just then four humans appeared in the door of the garage, all of them carrying large lumps of wood.

"Right! Do up your seat belt and hold on tight because we're getting out of here right now," shouted Brains to Muscles as he headed straight towards the enemy.

Muscles did as he was told but shut his eyes at the same time. He also kept his head down as best he could just in case the humans took a swing at them. Brains drove straight at the four in the doorway but chose his route very carefully. There were three men and one woman blocking their escape. Now Brains realized that the men might not move. This meant that they would be in deep trouble. But the woman was the same one that screamed a lot and also was scared of mice. So he headed straight for her legs. As soon as she realized what was happening, she screamed, dropped the lump of wood and ran for it. The lump of wood landed straight across the car and they nearly crashed, but Muscles grabbed hold of it and threw it at the three men that were chasing them. It hit one of them on the shin stopping him from chasing them anymore. He held his leg and screamed in agony. The other two men gave up as the little car and the two mice sped along the path and around the corner.

Chapter Four

Big Bad Fox

Round the corner and along the path they went as fast as the little car would go. Brains steered the best he could and changed gear when he thought he had to, such as slowing down to turn a corner or go around a tree. Muscles opened his eyes once but shut them again when he saw a tree looming towards them. Somehow Brains steered them around it, but Muscles decided to keep his eyes shut just in case. If he couldn't see things speeding towards them then surely he couldn't see if they hit them.

Brains realized that if they stayed on the same path they would go around the block and back to where they had come from. So he decided to cross the road. He didn't stop to look for traffic because he wasn't sure how to stop. He knew that he somehow had to take his foot off of one pedal and press another one downwards, but he wasn't sure which one or how hard to press. So he just turned the steering wheel towards the road and hoped for the best. He also closed his eyes as they bumped heavily down the kerb.

He opened his eyes when he heard a very loud horn. It was a lorry and this lorry was only yards away from them. Without even thinking what to do next, Brains stepped on one of the other pedals with his tiny foot. The little car came to a sudden stop just as the lorry reached them. There was a loud screech of brakes as the lorry tried to stop. Miraculously all those large lorry wheels missed them.

Brains put his foot down on the other pedal again, changing gears as they gained speed and went under the lorry, out the other side, up the kerb and back on to the path on the other side of the road, almost hitting a human on a bicycle. Muscles closed his eyes again but asked shakily if it was safe to open them.

"Of course it's safe. I'm getting the hang of this driving now," said Brains with a smile.

Soon the path ended and they were driving across a very large grassy area. It must be a park where families come to play. There were shrubs and flower beds. They could drive into one of them and hide if danger lurked nearby.

Muscles, who now had his eyes open, spotted a group of children on bicycles. They had spotted the mice and were cycling towards them. Some came from the right side and others from the left.

"Quick Brains, do something before they catch us!" yelled Muscles.

"I'm doing my best. Just hang on tight, I'll think of something," squeaked Brains as he headed for some shrubs. Then he realized that the children would jump off their bikes and search for them, so he skirted around the flower bed and headed for the exit.

The children cycled as fast as they could towards them. Some other children were now heading towards them too. This meant that the exit was blocked. What to do now? Brains did a sharp left turn and headed towards a hilly, lumpy part of the park.

Muscles didn't like this idea because the car might crash. But Brains knew that the children wouldn't be able to ride their bikes over the lumpy ground.

They were bouncing all over the place. Several times they nearly got thrown out of the car, but the seat belts helped them stay seated - just!

Just as they thought they might be safe, disaster struck. Brains was glancing behind when Muscles shouted to him to look in front. Almost too late Brains glanced to the front only to see a large rabbit eating some dandelion leaves directly ahead of them. With a quick turn of the wheel, they avoided the rabbit, missing him by inches. But they didn't miss the tree that was lurking nearby.

Crash went the little car. Crash, bang, wallop went Muscles and Brains as they bounced against their seat belts and then on to the seat again. They knew they had to get out quickly because they could hear the children shouting excitedly. They were very close by.

They undid the seat belts and scrambled out as fast as they could. The rabbit ran into its burrow in the side of a hill. "We sure scared him out of his wits. But where do we run to for safety?" cried Muscles.

"Follow me quickly. We'll have to hide in the rabbit's burrow until the children go away. Let's just hope the rabbits are friendly and don't mind us sharing their home for a short time." So they ran up the hill and leapt into the opening of the burrow just as the children arrived at their little car.

They heard a grown up talking to the children. He was telling them that there weren't any mice in the car. They must have imagined it. "Anyway, mice don't drive cars," he laughed.

Just then the two mice realized that the rabbit had come back to the entrance and was standing over them.

"What do you two want? What do you think you're doing? You could easily have killed me. And how did you learn to drive?" He asked lots and lots of questions, but he didn't give the mice a chance to answer. Eventually he stopped talking and looked at them. Then he blurted out, "Well, answer me. Who are you and where do you come from? Where are you going?"

Brains stepped forward and held up a paw.. "Stop, stop, stop!" he said. "We were being chased by human children and we needed to escape, so that's why I was driving that little car. I didn't see you until the last moment. I nearly got killed trying to miss you. Now the car is damaged and we're still not safe. We need somewhere safe to stay for a short time. Can you help us please?"

The rabbit told them to stay there while he

had a word with the other rabbits in the burrow. So off he hopped into the dark tunnel.

They took a peek out of the burrow to see if the humans were still there. Unfortunately, the children had picked up the little car and were examining it. Then they put it down again and started to search amongst the flowers and trees.

"They must be looking for us. Let's hope the rabbits come back soon," said Brains. Just then, out of the dark burrow hopped the bunny.

"OK, you two follow me. The others want to see you and talk to you."

So off they scurried trying to keep up with the rabbit. They went around a bend, then around another until they came to a large open area. There was some fur in one corner and some food in another. The two mice had come face to face with four more rather large rabbits.

"How can we help you?" asked one of the rabbits.

Brains explained their problem and said that a safe place to stay would be a big help. Also, a little bit of food if possible. After all, they were only small and didn't eat much.

The biggest rabbit stepped forward and

said, "Sorry, but we have our babies in these tunnels. We must protect them from any danger, they must come first. You aren't welcome here. Please go now."

"We aren't a danger to you or your families," protested Brains. But their protesting did no good at all. The rabbits started to move towards them. Now, Muscles knew that he might possibly beat a couple of them, but there were too many here now. Also, Brains would easily be beaten, maybe even killed, so they started to retreat towards another exit.

Just as they were about to leave they noticed a huge snout being pushed into the hole. The rabbits then all started to run the other way down the tunnel. The two mice followed them just to be on the safe side.

When they reached the open area again, one of the rabbits explained that the snout belonged to a fox. He came by every day about lunch time. The trouble was that one of them usually ended up being his lunch. They were afraid of him.

Brains had a quick whisper in Muscles' ear. He realized what they had to do to stay here for awhile. Muscles nodded to Brains.

"Right, listen up you cowardly rabbits. We can help you if you will let us stay for awhile."

"What can two small mice do for us?" growled the biggest rabbit. "You're too small and weak to be any good to anyone. What are you going to do, fight the fox perhaps?" he laughed.

Muscles and Brains quickly glanced at each other. They had a plan. Brains spoke quietly but with conviction.

"Yes, we'll fight the fox. We'll chase him away. Then perhaps you'll let us stay here tonight and have some food."

All of the rabbits burst out laughing. They just didn't believe a word that the two mice were saying.

"OK. Out you go and chase that big bad fox away," they chuckled. Brains didn't stop to listen to them for a second longer. He was very angry with the rabbits.

"Come on Muscles, let's show these scared rabbits how to tackle a fox." Then he whispered very quietly. "I hope you can handle him because if you don't do it right I'll be eaten."

"Don't worry," squeaked Muscles. "I can handle him easily."

Brains took a crafty look outside the burrow. The fox was a few yards away and had his snout down another burrow. Brains told

Muscles to follow him. They crept up behind the fox. Just as Muscles was about to grab his tail, the fox turned around. He must have sensed that there was danger about. The fox saw Brains run and tried to stop him with his paw. But while he was engrossed with Brains, Muscles had run around the other way and grabbed hold of the fox's tail. He then ran with his tail over his shoulder. The fox couldn't understand what was happening.

Muscles started to swing the fox around and around above his head. He then let him go and the fox flew through the air and landed in the branches of a tree.

The rabbits had been watching from several entrances to their burrow. They couldn't believe their eyes. Did that really happen, they thought?

The fox got down from the tree in a very dazed condition and when he saw the mice running towards him he soon made a dash for safety.

Now the rabbits were bounding out of the tunnels and dancing, sort of hop hop dancing around on the grass.

The largest one said, "Come on you two mice. Let's eat to celebrate and then find you some soft fur for a bed for the night."

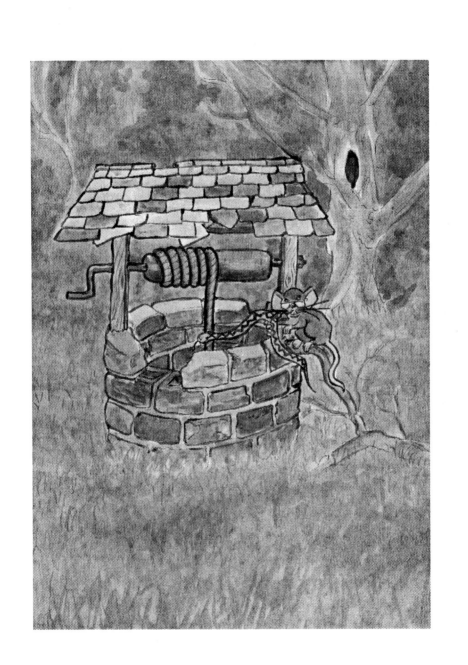

Chapter Five

Hungry Snake

The next morning they had a hearty breakfast and then Brains got Muscles to help him with the poor dented car. Muscles forced the bonnet open and Brains managed to fix the damage to the engine. After a couple of tries he got the engine going and they were ready to go. They thanked the rabbits for the bed and food and they were off again. They decided that what they both wanted was to find their family. They spotted a pigeon who gave them directions and they headed for Staines.

They kept to the country route whenever they could. This way they were less likely to be seen by humans.

The journey took them along country roads with high hedges and through lovely little villages. Sometimes they would have to pull off the road and hide because there were humans about. On one occasion they pulled into a farm gateway so they wouldn't be seen by a group of humans walking close by. But one of the children in the group wanted to investigate further when he thought he saw something move by the gate. They saw him walking towards them so Brains put his foot on the accelerator and sped off, but not before the child had spotted him.

He called to his friends to help find the mysterious little car that he had seen. They thought perhaps someone who lived on the farm was playing with a toy car, but after looking all around the buildings and inside those that weren't locked, they decided that their young friend had imagined the whole thing. Even though he said he was serious and he had seen the little car, they assumed that he was playing and he had only seen it in his mind. He wanted to have one more look for his imaginary car but they pulled him along and carried on with their walk. If only they knew the truth.

Muscles and Brains waited a few more minutes before surfacing from their hideaway. They took a good look around to make sure that the humans had gone before climbing out of the hole. They had to find something to eat and drink before going back to their car which was covered by straw. They just drove into a haystack in the corner of the barn, then ran and jumped into a hole that they had found. When they looked around the barn they found plenty of food to eat and there was water in a stream nearby. They ate and drank to their hearts content, then climbed back into the hole where they made a bed in the straw and promptly fell asleep. They were woken abruptly some time later. Brains opened his eyes to find a huge rat staring down at him. Muscles had the same view a few seconds later when he woke up.

"What do you think you're doing? Why have you made a bed in our tunnel? Why have you eaten our food?"

Questions, questions! "Get out now before we kill you," screamed the big rat who had now been joined by several more of his family.

Muscles and Brains tried to talk to them to explain why they were there, but the rats wouldn't listen to a word they said. They were pulled to the entrance of the tunnel and thrown out.

"Go away and never come back or we'll feed you to the snake. He can eat you instead of one of us," shouted another big rat.

Muscles would have fought back when they grabbed him to throw him out of the tunnel, but he decided to bide his time.

They were just about to go and get their car when one of the rats shouted, "Look out, here comes the snake!" The rats all dived into the hole as fast as they could go. They could run down the tunnels and out another hole somewhere outside of the barn. Sometimes the snake could get the right hole and catch one of the rats for lunch. However, this time he spotted the two mice sitting outside where the rats had thrown them.

"Looks like two mice for dinner. Makes a change from rat," giggled the snake as he slithered towards them.

Brains spoke quietly to Muscles. "Get ready - when you see me run, I think the snake will follow. Then it's up to you. If you get it wrong I'll be his lunch."

Just as the snake was almost upon them Brains ran straight past its head. He only just escaped as the snake lunged at him, missing him by inches. Brains kept on running as fast as his little legs would go. The snake could have gone for Muscles but decided to go after Brains instead. He almost had him the first time. Next time he would get him for sure. Too bad for him that as soon as he turned to follow Brains, Muscles leapt into action. He ran towards the snake and grabbed for his tail. He missed the first time because the snake was chasing Brains. The snake was determined to catch Brains and eat him and then he would come back for the other one.

But Muscles had other ideas. He leapt towards the snake's tail again and managed to grab hold this time. He pulled as hard as he could and swung the awful snake round and round in the air above his head. All the time he was doing this, he was walking towards a well that he spotted outside the barn. When he reached the well he threw the snake into it. Dow, down, down he went until he hit the water with a big splash.

"That's put paid to him," cheered Brains. "Thanks brother. We make a good team. But next time, get hold the first time, he nearly caught me." But Brains wasn't angry. He was laughing with excitement.

They were walking towards their car when a voice from behind them said, "How did you do that? You're so brave. Why not stop for awhile and tell us how you did it!" When they turned around they found one of the big rats standing there.

"We thought you wanted us to go," squeaked Brains. The rat told them that he had seen the whole thing and wanted to thank them both. He offered them food and a bed for as long as they wanted. They were very grateful and accepted the invitation graciously.

Over the next couple of days Muscles and Brains made sure that the little car was in good working order and filled their bellies with food offered by the rats.

Then one morning they put some food in the boot of the car just in case they had trouble finding more later. They said good-bye to the rats who had now become good friend. They realized how strong Muscles was and how intelligent Brains was with driving a car and everything. Finally, off they drove out of the barn through the gate and along the road in the direction of Staines.

Chapter Six

Airplane Adventure

Muscles and Brains drove for hours and hours. Every now and then they hid from humans that they came across. It was getting dark so they needed to find a place to stop. They saw a huge barn in a field and decided to take a look around. It could be a good place to rest for the night. So off they went, bump, bump, bump across the field.

It was very quiet. They began exploring to see if it was safe. There weren't any humans about and they couldn't even see any other creatures. They took the food out of the boot and hid the car in some hay they had found, then they carried the food into the barn. It seemed very big inside, probably because there was hardly anything in it, just a couple of dozen large boxes. They thought this very strange. Usually a barn like this would have bales of straw, old farm machinery and perhaps even a stable or two with horses in them. But this barn was almost empty.

They found some straw outside and took it into the barn to make a bed for themselves in a corner. When they finished that, they ate their food and then fell into a deep sleep.

They were awakened the next morning by the sound of human vehicles outside. They kept very quiet and listened. More vehicles were arriving and they could hear lots of human voices. That spelled danger for them. They crept toward the door but it was too late because humans were coming into the barn. They had to run and hide amongst the nearby boxes.

Muscles got the lid off one box and they climbed inside. They kept very still and quiet so that the humans wouldn't find them.

After awhile they got curious and wanted to see what was in the box. Muscles had no idea what it was, but Brains shouted, "It's a toy plane. It's a remote control toy plane! But what is it doing here?"

Just then the box started moving. One of the humans had picked it up and was carrying it across the barn. He put it down and started to take the lid off.

"Right," said Brains. "As soon as the lid comes off we'll make a run for it, try to get out of the barn and head for the car." Muscles wasn't going to argue. As soon as the lid came off they were gone, out of the box, across the barn floor and towards the door. There were lots of humans about, all with different types of remote control planes. What were they up to?

Muscles and Brains got through the door and were heading towards the straw where the car was hidden. All of a sudden Brains stopped running. Muscles bumped into him and said, "What's the matter? Why did you stop? We need to get into the car and get out of here."

But Brains just pointed to the pile of straw. A young human was playing in it - and he had their car. Brains was speechless. Even he didn't know what to do now. Muscles could try to get it back from the human, but if he did a lot of bigger humans were close, and if they helped the one small one with the car, then Muscles and Brains wouldn't have a chance.

Brains grabbed Muscles and told him they needed to hide until it was dark again and try to get their car back later. So they found a warm, quiet place and hid. They watched all day to see what was going on.

The humans were flying their planes here, there and everywhere. Brains reckoned that they were getting ready for a competition. At least they would be occupied and not be interested in a couple of little mice.

That night, just as it was getting dark, Muscles and Brains decided to go back into the barn to look for their car. Almost all of the humans had gone camping nearby. There were just a couple of them left behind in the barn to look after the planes overnight.

Muscles and Brains crept into the barn and started to search for their car. When they finally found it, they were horrified to find that all the wheels had been taken off. They searched and searched and eventually found two of them. Then Brains spotted the other two. They had been put on to one of the planes. He could get them back on the car easily enough, but Muscles would have to lift the car up while Brains put them on. The other two wouldn't be so easy. Brains had to try and get them off of the plane. But before he had a chance, he was disturbed by the two humans. They were checking all the planes with their torches. Muscles and Brains ran for cover as quickly and quietly as they possibly could. They watched from behind one of the boxes to see just what the humans were up to. They saw that they were damaging all of the planes. They weren't here to guard them at all. They were obviously making sure that their plane was going to win the competition.

Brains just had to do something abut this. He told Muscles to get into the passenger seat of one of the planes.

"What good will that do?" moaned Muscles.

"You'll see. Just get into one that isn't damaged."

"Which one?" Muscles moaned again.

"I'll check them first. While I do that, you can open the barn door a bit more. Do it quietly so the humans won't hear."

Before Muscles could answer, Brains set about checking for a plane that wasn't damaged. A few minutes later Brains found him with his head in a plane's engine compartment. "This is the one," he said excitedly. "Get in and sit still."

Muscles climbed into the passenger seat. "I wonder what he's up to now. Always fiddling with things. We should be getting out of here, not waiting around to get caught." Lots of thoughts were going through his mind.

Just then Brains climbed in next to him. "Right, let's get going," squeaked Brains.

"Good idea and about time too," replied Muscles just as he was about to climb out of the plane.

"What are you doing? Where are you going?" snapped Brains. Muscles just looked at him.

He said, "Please tell me you aren't going to try to fly this thing." Please tell me I'm wrong!" He was very frightened.

"Don't be silly. We'll be fine. You did open the door a bit more didn't you?"

By now Muscles was too scared to talk and too scared to move. He could only manage a little nod of his head.

The two humans shined the torch straight at them. "Stop that plane right now! Get it! We have to turn the engine off!" said one of them. He grabbed the remote control and tried to stop the plane but Brains had bypassed the controls. HE was now in charge of the plane. They glided around the barn a couple of times and then into the air just in time because the humans were right in front of them. Brains pulled the right lever and the plane soared over the humans and headed for the door.

"Muscles! I thought you opened the door a bit more!" groaned Brains as he looked ahead of him. He wasn't sure there was enough room to fly through but it was too late to turn the plane around now.

"I didn't know you were going to fly out. I thought we were going to run for it. There won't be enough room for this plane to fly through. Can't you stop it?" cried a very frightened, wide eyed Muscles. But there wasn't any time left. They both shut their eyes as they approached the door at a very fast speed. Brains could feel the night breeze on his face. He opened his eyes and was relieved to find that somehow they had made it. They were out of the barn and still in the air.

There were lights in the field. That must be where the other humans were camping. Brains turned the plane towards them. As soon as he approached the lights he could see humans looking up into the sky. They heard the plane and were looking for it. They knew that no one should be flying after dark.

Muscles had opened his eyes now and was shouting to Brains. "Not that way! I'm sure the barn is the other way. Turn around and let's get out of here!" But Brains was determined to get the humans to go after him. He wanted them to go to the barn and find the other two humans that had damaged their planes.

The group of humans that followed him were

surprised to find the other two humans coming out of the barn. They would have a lot of explaining to do. After a couple of times around the barn, Brains circled low over the heads of the humans before flying off in what he hoped was the direction of Staines.

"Hold on tight Muscles. Staines - here we come!" And off they flew.

Chapter Seven

Home At Last

Muscles and Brains woke up the next morning feeling very refreshed and ready to go. They ate some breakfast and drank from a nearby stream before heading towards the plane.

The twigs and leaves they had covered it with had been blown away by the strong weather, otherwise it seemed OK. Muscles was a bit worried about the wind, but Brains didn't seem to notice it much.

They climbed aboard and started the engine. They moved along the ground slowly, then faster and faster, then Brains said, "Hold on tight, here we go." They lifted off the ground and up into the sky. After they had been airborne for awhile Brains checked to see if they were going in the right direction. He had spotted some swans flying not far away, so he headed towards them and joined the flock alongside the lead swan.

"Can you tell us if we're gong the right way for Staines, please?" he asked politely.

"Just follow us. We're going to land on the Thames by Staines Bridge. Just fall in behind but be careful. The wind is very strong today," replied the swan in a very friendly tone.

So they dropped back behind the swans and followed them the best they could. The wind kept blowing the plane all over the place and Brains struggled to keep flying as straight as possible.

A message was passed along the line of swans until the one nearest to Muscles and Brains said, "That's the Thames up ahead. If you lose us, just head for it. If you keep flying just follow the river until you pass a park with a swimming pool. The park is on the left. Then there is an island in the river with some houses on it. About two minutes past the island is a bridge over the river. That's Staines Bridge. We're stopping there for a few days. We get fed by the humans every day.

Just then the wind blew extra hard. The plane was being blown away from the swans. Brains had a terrible job keeping them from crashing. He held on and kept aiming towards the river. Muscles had his eyes well and truly closed. Closer and closer they got to the river, but unfortunately, they were losing altitude very quickly. Then Brains told Muscles to open his eyes. He needed him to keep a lookout for the park, the island or, better still, the bridge.

Suddenly, Muscles screamed with excitement. "There's an island ahead. It has a park just before it and there's a childrens swimming pool in the park. There's a large flat area of ground. Can you land there before we crash?"

Brains saw all of this and tried to steer the plane towards the park. But the wind was too strong and they were being blown past the park and then past the island.

"I can see the bridge," screamed Muscles. "We're nearly home. The plane was being blown all over the place. Poor Brains had almost no control at all but he kept on trying. He was doing his very best. All of a sudden the wind dropped. It had almost completely died down. Only for a moment or two but enough time for the plane to hit the water, out of control. Brains realized that they were sinking fast. They had to get out and swim to the river bank if they could.

Muscles dived into the water with Brains close behind. They were swimming as fast as they could but the river was running faster and they were struggling hard. Just then Muscles saw a fish swimming towards them. Perhaps he would help them get to the river bank.

Brains also spotted a fish and now he really was in a blind panic. This fish wouldn't help them. It was a large Pike and he knew that Pike ate other creatures as well as other fish. He shouted to Muscles, "It'll eat us if it gets close enough. Swim faster, save yourself brother!"

Muscles couldn't leave his brother to die. He had to do his best to save both of them. So he turned around to swim back toward Brains. He couldn't see him, he had vanished completely. Muscles assumed that the Pike had eaten Brains and he started to swim towards the fish. He intended to fight to avenge his brother's death. But before he reached him, he suddenly rose out of the water. He didn't understand just what had happened until he landed softly on a bed of white feathers. Sitting next to him was Brains, soaking wet and frightened but safe.

"Where are we?" asked Muscles. "What happened? I thought the fish had eaten you."

Then he realized that they were still on the river. Only now they were sailing along on the back of a swan. The swan spoke to them in a lovely soft voice. He said, "I saw your plane heading towards the river and followed it. I guessed you might need a bit of help, so here I am. You're safe now. I'll take you to where we get fed. It's just the other side of the bridge."

Muscles and Brains sat very still and quietly until they were ready to jump from the swan's back on to dry land. They thanked him very much for all the wonderful help he had given them. He had saved their lives. The swan grabbed a couple pieces of bread that had been thrown out by the humans.

"Here," he said. "You must be hungry. I can get plenty more."

Once again they thanked him. They took the bread and headed for the safety of the shrubbery by the bridge. They were home and they were safe. Well, safe as any mouse can be.

Chapter Eight

Over The Bridge

Now that Muscles and Brains had arrived back in Staines, they wanted to find their parents again.

For a few days and nights now the two mice had been staying under Staines Bridge. During the day, they managed to collect some of the food that the humans fed to the ducks and swans. At night they slept in a bed made from feathers that they had gathered along the river bank. This bed was hidden in a dark corner underneath the bridge. One night they were attacked by some vicious rats who had decided to kick the newcomers out, but Muscles soon got involved and after throwing one over the head of the other and sent one sailing through the air after swinging him around by his tail, the rats knew they had to leave these two mice alone.

Now Muscles and Brains began the search for their family. Brains suggested finding some other mice and asking them for some help. The swan who had helped save their lives during their journey home had suggested where they might find other mice, so after thanking him, off they went.

To start with, they crossed the river by using the bridge. At night it would be safer, or at least they thought it should have been. But nothing is easy for these two. Just as they were about half way across, they spotted a human. Not just any human, but one with two dogs. Neither of the two dogs was on a lead. Brains shouted to Muscles to run for cover. Too late! The dogs had spotted them. They were soon being chased over the bridge to where they had started.

They ran down the steps to a large patch of undergrowth in the hope of escaping from the beastly dogs. But they soon realized that they were still being followed. The human was calling the dogs to heel, but they were not listening.

Muscles told Brains to keep running while he dealt with the dogs. He found a branch that had been broken from a tree and then hid in the shrub. Just as the first dog reached him, he jumped out and swung the branch at the dog's front legs. Then he hit him over the head with the branch. The dog soon got up and ran back to his owner whimpering. The other dog saw what had happened and had the sense to turn back before he got hit as well. Muscles dropped the branch and ran after Brains.

A short while later Muscles and Brains were on their way over the bridge again. Only this time they made sure that there was no one about at all.

They soon reached the place that the swan had told them about. It was a pub with a cellar underneath. That's where they were expecting to find a family of mice.

They searched around for an entrance and soon found a hole underneath the fence and the cellar door was about two inches above the ground. They easily got into that.

Just as they were looking around for other mice, Brain suddenly stopped in his tracks.

"See that food on the lump of wood?" he said in a very worried voice. "Well, it's a trap. If you touch the food a metal bar will fall on you, then you either die straight away or die slowly in agony. Humans have put it there to catch mice like us."

Muscles understood the danger and decided

to put the trap out of order. But before he got to it, another mouse ran out from behind a case of beer and headed towards it.

"Keep away from our food," shouted the new mouse. He was just about to grab the food in his mouth when Muscles leapt into action just in time. The trap was seconds away from crushing the poor creature's head. Soon all three of them were eating the food left on the trap. Muscles had broken the metal bar so that it couldn't harm them any more. The new mouse was very grateful and said he would take Muscles and Brains to his family. He also said that several of them had been killed by the humans recently because they didn't understand how dangerous these traps were.

First of all, he showed them where other traps were hidden around the cellar. Muscles soon put them out of action. Then they gathered up all the spare food and followed their new found friend to his family. They lived in a disused caravan. They had found a mattress inside and had gathered lots of stuffing to make a lovely warm, comfortable home for themselves. Muscles and Brains were soon made welcome by this new family, especially as they had taken them a gift of food. They were invited to stay for as long as they wanted and they could use this as their home while searching for their own family.

There were six mice living here at the moment, Mum, Dad and four children, two boys and two girls. Muscles and Brains couldn't believe how good looking the girls were. Their names were Mary and Jane Cooper, the two boys were called John and Mike but everyone called the parents Mum and Dad. So Muscles and Brains did the same.

Every day new traps would be found and every day Muscles broke them. He often wondered what the humans would think. Then one day he found out.

He was in the cellar with his new family when Jane cried out to him. She was trapped, but he knew he had made all the traps safe. He ran to where he heard her voice, then his heart sank to his feet. Jane was trapped but not in the usual type of gadget. She was in a small cage. She had walked into it and picked up the food. When she did this, the door slammed shut on her. She was not hurt at all, just frightened and Muscles knew he could get her out easily enough. All he had to do was climb on top and pull the door up. But just as he was going to do that, he heard the cellar door open.

He called to Brains to quickly think of a plan. In a matter of seconds Brains had an idea. He told Muscles to get the cage out of site.

Muscles picked the cage with Jane in it and ran behind a beer barrel.

"Now wait for my word and then do as I tell you." shouted Brains. The human had come down to the cellar to change a barrel. She had to go through a door into the chilled part of the cellar to do this. As soon as she went through the door, Brains called to Muscles.

"Now quickly push one of those new barrels in front of the door. Quickly, before she tries to come out again. We have only a couple of minutes."

Muscles was soon pushing with all of his might. He soon had a barrel in place.

"I think I'll put another one there to be on the safe side," he squeaked. He was pleased that the barrels had been delivered earlier that day and had not been put away yet. In no time at all he had Jane out of the cage and safely back with Mum and Dad.

The human lady took at least five minutes to get free. She ran up the stairs screaming at the other humans. Apparently she thought they had played a trick on her. They will never know the truth will they?

Brains spent a lot of time explaining all about the two types of traps that were being used. Also, how NOT to get caught. But in his heart, he knew that sooner or later they would either forget his advice or the humans would devise another way to catch them.

Over the next few weeks, the two brothers toured all over the area looking for their parents but no one seemed to know them. They loved staying with their new family but wanted to "go home." The only thing that stopped them leaving was Mary and Jane. The two brothers had fallen in love with them.

Chapter Nine

The Kestrel And The Cat

They had met with a few different families of mice during their two weeks on this side of the river. Lovely, friendly families but no one knew where their own family lived.

One day as they collected food on the bank of the Thames, Brains came up with an idea. They had only asked other mice for help. But perhaps they should ask other creatures as well. They asked swans, geese, moorhens and even seagulls, plus many other friendly creatures. They asked as many as they could but the answer was always the same; no one knew where they could find their family.

Muscles and Brains decided that they had to get on with their lives. They settled down to a normal every day routine. The only difference was that Mary and Jane were always near them.

One evening they went for a stroll on to Staines Bridge. They wanted to show the girls the wonderful view along the river. It is truly beautiful, especially when you're in love as these two were.

They were looking between the railings over the river when disaster struck. A Kestrel had seen Jane and decided that dinner was waitng in the form of a mouse. He swooped down and grabbed her in his claws, then dipped toward the river.

Muscles saw what was happening and dived off the bridge with one huge leap. He managed to grab hold of one of the Kestrel's tail feathers, then he swung himself up on to the bird's back between his wings.

"Now you let go of my friend," he shouted. "If you don't let go I'll pull all of your wing feathers off and you won't be able to fly."

The Kestrel knew that he had no choice but to obey. But he wasn't going to give in that easily. He did a roll over to try to make Muscles fall into the river. But Muscles hung on to the bird's feathers. Then he pulled out a large wing feather.

"Ouch, that hurt!" squawked the Kestrel. He knew he was beaten so dropped Jane into the river. Muscles dived in after her. He wanted to make sure that she got to the river bank safely. Jane managed to grab hold of a lump of wood that was floating down the river. Muscles swam over to her and helped her climb on top of the wood, then he swam and pushed until they were bumping along the river bank. Jane jumped onto the grassy verge and Muscles was soon clambering up beside her. He was pleased to see that she was only shaken and otherwise unharmed.

The Kestrel hovered overhead knowing he was beaten, so he flew away, probably to feed further along the river bank.

Soon Brains and Mary were running towards Muscles and Jane along the path.

"Well done Muscles. You saved my sister's life," Mary said gratefully. Then she put her arms around him and gave him a big kiss on the cheek. He blushed bright red and then said, "Well, I do love her very much, so I couldn't let her be eaten by the Kestrel could I!?" He blushed even more when he realized just what he had said; so did Jane when she heard him.

When they had rested for awhile, they decided to get back home to tell Mary and Jane's Mum and Dad all about their adventure. Because they had got out of the river on the opposite side from Staines, they had to go over the bridge again to get home. Brains had a wonderful idea and sat down to tell them.

"I'm still exhausted from my swim," he said. "I don't think I can make it all the way home." He told Muscles that he had seen an old skateboard underneath the arches of the bridge, it must have been thrown there by some humans.

Muscles lifted it over this head and carried it up all those steps. He put it on the path and went back for Jane. She was doing her best to climb to the top of the steps and Mary and Brains were helping her. They all reached the top and Muscles told them to get onto the skateboard. He was helping Jane climb aboard when Brains suddenly shouted, "Watch out Muscles. Behind you. Give us a push, quickly!"

Muscles glanced behind him only to see a huge cat bounding in his direction. He gave the skatboard one hefty push and at the same time jumped on board.

The cat was chasing them at a fair old speed, but they too were moving very fast. Over the bridge and down the other side they went with the cat hot on their heels. He had almost caught up with them when they reached the far side of the bridge where the road splits. One way goes round to the right and the other goes straight ahead. They had no control over the skateboard. They had no means of turning corners so they had to go straight ahead. Down the kerb and into the road! A car was coming but they were safely halfway across; the cat wasn't. The car saw him and tried to swerve out of his way. Why he wasn't run over no one knew. Talk about using up one of his nine lives!

"I honestly thought he was a goner then," squeaked Mary with a giggle.

"So did I," laughed Jane.

Muscles and Brains thought the daft cat would have given up after that close call, but oh no!! He was still after them and getting closer with every second that passed.

While all of this was going on, Brains had been busy. He had been undoing the back wheels of the skateboard. It was difficult but he was doing it all the same. You see, he had a plan, good old Brains.

They were getting very close to where they lived and would soon need to stop the skateboard. Brains had worked out a way to stop the cat and the skateboard at the same time. He had told the others to be ready and when he shouted, "Now!" they all scrambled to the front of the board. Of course, now that the rear wheels were no longer attached, the front lifted a few inches into the air. As the rear wheels got a little further behind Brains shouted, "Now!" again. They followed him. Only this time to the back end. The board dropped to the ground and acted like a brake. The loose wheels hit the board and bounced back towards the cat. He saw them coming towards him but too late to get out of the way. He was rammed by the loose wheels and knocked for six. Meanwhile, the four mice were running into the pub and to the safety of their home. Mum and Dad were pleased to see them home unharmed, especially their two daughters.

Chapter Ten

Ponies, Boats and Golf Balls

"We have to look in another part of Staines for our family," said Brains one lovely morning. "They aren't anywhere that we have looked so far," was Muscles' reply.

So after breakfast they set out on their travels again They had eaten well because the cook had prepared too much food for the pub. The leftovers were thrown into the rubbish bag and put in the yard. They soon had the bag opened and found lots to eat.

Now they headed towards the big park with the swimming pool that they passed when they were trying to get to Staines in the airplane. They stopped in the church yard opposite the park because there were a lot of humans around. The humans seemed to be having a special day in the park. They were playing tennis, crazy golf and ponies were giving the children rides. Some went around the children's play area while others walked down to the river and back. It is amazing how humans find so much spare time to enjoy themselves.

In the church yard the mice met a family of field mice. They were very friendly and said they would help Muscles and Brains if they could. They knew of several mice families that lived on the far side of the park.

They all decided that the quickest way was to cross the park. It would be dangerous because of all the humans around, but they felt that there was enough shelter for them to hide if they had to. So off they went, through the hedge and on to the crazy golf course. Muscles and Brains told the field mice to go around the edge for safety. But, one of the youngsters wandered on to one section where the humans were playing and Brains shouted to him to watch out as he had spotted a golf ball rolling towards him and he pushed him into the hole, the one where the ball is supposed to go. Unfortunately, the ball followed them in. Muscles spotted it in time and punched it out of the way before it could land on top of them.

The look on the faces of the humans was incredible. They couldn't understand what was happening. They started to walk towards the hole so Brains called out to Muscles and the little mouse to run for their lives.

Out they both popped and started to run. They didn't now which way was best, so they headed towards the ponies. The humans saw them and decided that their game had been ruined, so they gave chase as fast as they could. One of them started to throw golf balls at the two mice, but that was a big mistake. Muscles stopped running, got hold of the golf balls and started to throw them back at the humans.

"That will teach them a lesson," he mumbled as he turned and ran after his field mouse companions. By now, they had all met up again near the pony rides. Several of the ponies were grazing while others were taking riders back and forth around the park.

Brains approached one of them and asked, "Can you help me please? I am trying to find my parents. I think they might be on the other side of the park."

The pony was lovely and polite and said that if they would climb on to his back he would take them across the park.

Just as they settled, (some in his mane,

some in his tail), a human plonked a child into the saddle and pulled his reins over his head.

"Come on, giddy-up. That's enough, rest for now," the human growled at the pony. He tried to get him to go one way but the pony knew he had to go the other way for the mice, but he was tugged and pulled all over the place. But still he tried to go the right way for the mice.

Eventually, Muscles finally had enough. Fortunately, so had the child's parents. They grabbed the child and walked away moaning loudly, "Bad tempered ponies. Too dangerous by far," and lots of other mumbling.

While this was going on Muscles grabbed the reins from the human's hand, jumped on to the pony's back and shouted, "Let's go pony. Run for all you're worth!"

Now the pony knew that he would be told off for doing this but he just wanted to help his new friends. So off he ran,, scattering humans all over the place. His owner was running after him but not nearly fast enough.

All of the mice were glad to be back on the ground again. They had been bumped and shaken all over the place, but at least they were on the other side of the park at last. The pony's owner caught him up just as he began to graze on a large patch of green grass. He assumed that was why the pony had run off.

The mice searched around for a long time until eventually they found other mice. They weren't sure about this invasion of strangers, but Brains soon convinced them that they meant no harm. Unfortunately, the new mice didn't know Muscles and Brains family. But they invited them to stay for tea. It should be safer to cross the park again later when most of the humans had gone home.

They followed the new mice back into the park to find something to eat. The rubbish bins don't always get emptied so there should be plenty of food in them. Humans do waste so much but mice don't - nor do rats unfortunately. As soon as the mice tried to feed from one of the bins, out jumped a huge rat. He tried to bite Brains. Fortunately, his mouth was full of chips and he couldn't get any more into it. Then along came five more of his family. These rats were much bigger than all the mice, so they didn't stand much of a chance. They all turned and ran. Even Muscles was legging it as fast as he could. How strange!

But the rats made a big mistake this time. Muscles had spotted a child's golf club that must have been dropped earlier. He picked it up in his tiny paws and waited for the rats. Brains had told the new mice to go home. He took them back to the church yard while Muscles kept the rats at bay.

Muscles was swinging the golf club at the legs of the rats. After he knocked two of them over, the rest turned and ran away. He spotted the mouse family disappearing, so he ran after them and Brains. They were heading towards the river so he followed them.

Brains told them to follow the path by the river. This went all the way to the gate opposite the church yard. But they were in for a nasty shock. As if from out of nowhere came a huge cat. They only spotted it because of the bell that it had around its neck. He started chasing them towards the river. Just as they were on the edge, he caught one of them in his huge paws. Terrified, the rest of the mice jumped into the river.

Muscles was soon running towards the huge monster. He wanted to save his friend from a certain nasty death. He still had the child's golf club in his paws. He swung at the cat and caught him on the chin, more by luck than anything. He swung again and this time caught him on the paw that was holding the mouse.

Immediately the mouse was dropped and running towards the river.

They ran to the river's edge and were amazed to see a remote control boat waiting for them. Brains was steering it along the river wall. The two mice jumped on board just in time. The huge cat was almost upon them. Muscles pushed off from the bank and they were away. The cat tried to reach them and fell into the water. He was last seen trying to scramble out, soaking wet and angry. They all laughed and said it served him right.

As they were going along the river in the boat, Brains explained that when he jumped into the water to escape from the cat, he saw the boat in the reeds on the other side of the river by the island. So he swam over to it and realized that he could start it without much trouble. What a good idea this was.

When they reached the bridge that joins the island to the river bank, Brains pulled over and got out of the boat. He tied it to a branch that was hanging down almost touching the water. Then the others got out and headed for the church yard. Fortunately, they only had a little way to go because the cat had scrambled out of the water and was following them.

Muscles told the others to run back while he

handled this determined nuisance of a cat. They all ran through the church gate and into their house where it was safe. Muscles hid on the other side of the gate. When the cat came close enough, with one almighty push the gate caught him head on. The poor thing was stunned and knocked right on to his back. Muscles headed toward the others and into a warm bed for the night.

Chapter Eleven

Under And Out

The next morning they got up early and said goodbye to their new found friends. Muscles and Brains went back to the boat and headed for Staines Bridge. Mary and Jane decided to go with them.

The wind was very strong this morning and the water was very choppy. Water kept getting into the boat. The trees were blowing in the wind and the branches seemed even more menacing as they bowed and dipped with each gust.

Suddenly, a large branch snapped from an old tree and crashed down towards the water. Unfortunately, it landed on top of the boat. "Thwack" it went and the boat broke in two throwing the four of them into the fast flowing water.

Muscles was a fast, strong swimmer which

was just as well. He spotted Brains trying to get to the bank but he could see that he was struggling to stay afloat. The two girls were nowhere to be seen. Muscles swam over to Brains and helped him get to safety. Then he swam back to where the two halves of the boat were and started searching for Mary and Jane. He dived under the water again and again but couldn't find them. He finally swam back to Brains. He was exhausted. Just as they climbed on to the river bank up popped Ted and Tina Tern. They are birds that live on the river. They dive down to the bottom for their food and pop back up yards and yards away. This time when they popped up, Muscles noticed that they each had a passenger on their neck. One had Mary and the other had Jane clinging on to them for dear life.

Very soon the two lady mice were laying on the bank exhausted. Ted and Tina had seen them struggling and sinking, so they dived down to save them. That's what friends are for.

The mice thanked them for their help and the Terns disappeared as quickly as they had arrived, under the water for food.

When everyone had recovered from their ordeal, they went back to the caravan where

Mary and Jane's family lived. They would have something to eat before getting a good night's sleep.

Early next morning they were woken by the sound of humans. They were clearing everything out of the caravan. As quietly as they could the mice slipped out of their beds and through the hole they had made in the floor. Now they only had to drop down to the ground to safety.

Muscles and Brains made sure that every mouse was out before making a run for it. They decided to head towards a little river that flows into the big one that runs under Staines Bridge. But the humans had discovered them and gave chase. Two of them had nets so they must have realized the mice were in the caravan.

Mary, Jane and their mother were trapped against a wooden fence and one human with a net was only feet away.

Brains saw that the fence was old and the wooden slats were loose, but they were still too heavy for him to move. So he called out to Muscles for help. In a matter of seconds the fence slats were moving. Muscles had made a gap big enough for the mice to get through. By the time the humans got around the fence, every mouse had disappeared.

Not long after their lucky escape, the mice were standing on the rocks that were part of the bank by the little river. They were looking for a safe place to make a new home for themselves when they spotted two ducks nearby. Brains called out asking them if they could perhaps tell him where would be the safest place to make their new home.

The drake began squawking loudly and flapping his wings as he ran across the top of the water towards them.

"Get away from here, stay away from us," he kept shouting at them. "If you go near our nest you'll be in serious trouble."

So the mice went further along the river bank and out of the ducks way. Brains realized that something must have upset them very badly for them to be so aggressive.

It was while they were heading toward where the rivers joined that they met up with the friendly swan. He was pleased to see them again but disappointed that they hadn't found their family yet. He was still doing his bit to help by keeping his ears and eyes open. Any new mice for miles around were always asked if they knew the Penmouse family, but no luck so far.

When Brains asked why the drake was so nasty he was very upset with the answer the swan gave him. Apparently some humans had climbed down from the bridge over the little river and taken some eggs from the drakes nest. His partner was frightened off the nest after being threatened with sticks and stones. Now they had more eggs and just wanted everyone to keep away from them.

They found a nice place to rest and decided to make a little home under some rocks on the rivers edge. This would do for a few days until they moved on again. So they started searching for feathers, old wool and any other material that they could find.

It was just starting to get dark when they realized that they had not eaten supper. So off they went in search of food. They knew not to go too near the ducks nest. Just then, Muscles spotted two young humans climbing down by the bridge. The drake had spotted them too and was determined to defend his partner, the nest and, of course, the eggs. But Brains could see that the drake had no chance against the sticks and stones being thrown at him. He tried his best but was slowly being forced away from the nest. All the time he was getting hit, he still tried to fight back, but still they forced him further and further away.

Brains told Muscles that he was going to get their friend the swan and ask him to help. So off he went as fast as his little legs would go.

Muscles told Mary and Jane to hide while he did his best to help the poor drake. As they headed for the safety of their nest, Muscles was on his way towards the two young humans. They didn't see him sneak round behind them. He picked up a large stick,(large for a little mouse) and then walked up to about arms length from them, then he swung the stick with all his might and caught one of them on the back of his leg. It made the human jump with fright and he held his leg as he screamed. When he turned around he could see no one. Muscles had hidden behind a rock. The stick was laying on the ground so the human probably thought that someone else had thrown it at him. When he turned towards the drake again Muscles came out of hiding, grabbed the stick again and hit the other human. Only the stick broke. So he picked up some stones and started to throw them.

Unfortunately, the two humans started to retaliate. They picked up bigger stones than

Muscles could possibly cope with but he was determined not to be beaten.

Just as he thought his time was up, he heard an awful commotion coming from just around the bend of the river. The two humans heard it as well and turned to see where the noise was coming from.

When they saw the source of the commotion, they panicked big time. There were five swans flapping and squawking as they ran along the top of the water towards them. The humans dropped the stones and ran towards the bridge and in no time at all they were up, over and gone. When they were out of sight, Brains and the drake thanked the swans for their help. The nest was safe for now at least.

The next morning they met the drake who was feeding near his nest. He was very happy because the eggs had started to hatch. Once again he thanked the mice for all their wonderful help in saving his partner and their eggs.

When he asked them where they came from he was surprised to hear them say Staines as he didn't recognize them. Then they told him that they were looking for their family. When they mentioned their family name, the drake smiled. Then he said, You must be the two youngsters that got taken away in a tea chest. How did you manage to survive?"

When asked, he said he remembered the day they got taken away. He was flying with his partner and they were heading for the river when suddenly they spotted several mice on the ground. They seemed very distressed, so he and his partner stopped to see what was wrong. They were told that the mice had not been able to rescue all of their children and two had been taken away with a lot of furniture. They were in a nest in a tea chest in a garden shed at a house in Staines. The mice had managed to save the others but not the weakest two. They were very upset and didn't expect the two youngsters to survive. Obviously they had.

Muscles and Brains were getting very excited.

"Put me down you over strong oaf!" squeaked Brains as Muscles lifted him high into the air.

"Do you remember where you saw them?" questioned Brains. "We have searched all over Staines but no one there seems to know them."

The drake said that he knew exactly where he saw them. "It's in Staines but not exactly," he said. He went on to explain that, "Staines is this side of the river but also part over there is also Staines." He pointed across the river. He said that when the chicks had left the next he would be able to risk leaving them and then he could show the mice where he saw their family.

Muscles and Brains agreed to stay in their nest on the river bank until the ducks could all swim in the river. This took a few days as they didn't all hatch at the same time. But soon the drake said that he was ready to leave his young alone. He wouldn't be away long and the swans promised to keep an eye on them for him.

There were a lot of humans on the bridge, and lots of cars and lorries on the roads. So the drake suggested that as they couldn't fly, the mice should cross the river by taxis. By this he meant hitch a lift by swan or goose. He was sure that they would help out.

So off they went to the big river, one drake and eight mice all in a row. When they arrived they saw some swans and geese being fed bread by a family of humans. A little further along they saw two young boys fishing.

Suddenly, Brains called to Muscles, "Those two boys fishing are the same two that attacked the drake's nest. Be careful, I don't trust them."

When all the bread had been eaten and the

swans and geese began to move away, the drake jumped in amongst them. He asked several swans to help ferry the mice to the other side of the river. Very soon they were climbing on to the backs of the swans who raised their wings in an arch to safeguard the mice.

"Don't want you falling into the river do we?" said one very large swan. (The next time you see a swan with its wings up in an arch, just imagine that it may be taking some mice across the river). They were soon on their way with the drake out in front. It took four swans to help them, two mice to each swan.

Before they had gone very far though, one of the swans let out an awful squawk. He had been hit by something. It had landed across his back. It was the work of the two nasty young humans again. They had put a heavy weight on their fishing line about four inches from the hook. The weight had carried the line across the swan's back and one boy pulled his line in. The hook caught in the swan's feathers. He was in pain and being pulled towards the bank where the boys were. Suddenly, another swan screamed out. This time the weight had landed on his back and when it was pulled, the hook sunk into the swan's neck. Now they were both being dragged along towards the bank. The two boys were shouting with excitement. Muscles and Brains were on the second swan when all of this was happening.

Muscles knew that he had to do something to help the swans. Brains told him to pull the fishing line towards him so that he could get the hook out of the bird's neck. This had to be done very carefully so as not to hurt the swan.

When Muscles got the hook out he asked the swan to get as close as he possibly could to the swan who had the hook attached to his feathers. Muscles and Brains swapped places with two other mice. Now they could get that hook released as well. By now they were almost at the river bank and Brains had already devised a plan to get even with the two boys once and for all.

Muscles had one hook and line while Brains had the other. Both, of course, were attached to the lines which were on the two boys' fishing poles.

When they were close enough to the river bank they both jumped ashore. The two boys didn't see them because they thought the hooks were still stuck in the swans necks. They just kept reeling in their lines. Beside them were two big sticks. Obviously, they were going to hit the swans with them when they got close enough. But Muscles and Brains had other ideas. As soon ss they were on the river bank they ran between the boys' legs. The boys spotted them but too late to stop the fishing lines from being tightened around their legs. In no time at all the boys fell to the ground all tied up. Now was the time to get going. Muscles and Brains jumped back on to the swans and made their way to the other side of the river in double quick time. They thanked the swans for all their help and continued on their way.

By now the drake was waddling along the path towards the bridge. "Come on you lot. I haven't got all day you know. Got to get back to my missus and chicks soon.

They quickly caught him up just as he was going up a steep slope towards the road. When they reached the top which was quite a climb for a drake, he told them that it would best if he took just Muscles and Brains, then he could fly with them on his back. So the other six went into the undergrowth on the side of the path and headed for the safety of the arches under the bridge. Brains told them how to get to the nest that they had made some while ago when they lived there.

Then Muscles and Brains climbed back onto the drake and held tight as he took off.

"Not far to go, but too far to walk," squawked the drake. "Look down there. Can you see that shed? That's the garden where I saw them. We'll land there on the grass."

Just as they landed, they saw something move under the edge of one of the two sheds at the bottom of the garden. Then they saw a couple of mice coming towards them. They had recognized the drake and were coming to say hello. Muscles and Brains had not been spotted yet as they were still tucked under the feathers on the drakes' back.

The drake told the two mice from under the shed that he had a surprise for them.

"Okay you two, come on down and meet your parents!" he squawked happily.

Muscles and Brains were down on the ground in seconds and were hugging their parents. They knew they were really home at last.

The drake flew back to his family while Muscles and Brains took their parents down to the river to see their new mice friends, especially Mary and Jane. Muscles and Brains were happy that their family was together again. They introduced their new family to their old family and to their other new friends.

There were a few brothers and sisters they had not met before. They just knew there were many new adventures waiting for them as they lived and played with their friends and large family at home in Staines.

Printed in the United Kingdom
by Lightning Source UK Ltd.
107548UKS00002B/367-390